Christmas Fairy

Hello, fairy fans!

My name's Twink and I go to Glitterwings Academy, the most
amazing school you could possibly imagine. It's a magical school,
located in an oak tree in a glade of flowers, and it's where we
fairies learn how to fly, use fairy dust and care for animals.
If this sounds like your kind of place, you'll love reading about
the adventures my friends and I have at Glitterwings Academy.
And once you've finished this story, turn to the very back for fun
fairy activities, and to see all my glimmery Glitterwings Academy
books.

The festive story you're about to read takes place during the
winter holidays, when I met humans, tasted chocolate and
discovered the magic of Christmas for the very first time.
I hope you find it just as exciting as I did.

Lots of love,

Twink x

Christmas Fairy

Titania Woods

Illustrated by Smiljana Coh

BLOOMSBURY
CHILDREN'S
BOOKS

First published in Great Britain in 2008 by Bloomsbury Publishing Plc
36 Soho Square, London, W1D 3QY

A CIP catalogue record of this book is available from the British Library

ISBN 978 0 7475 9835 0

All papers used by Bloomsbury Publishing are natural, recyclable products made
from wood grown in well-managed forests. The manufacturing processes conform to
the environmental regulations of the country of origin.

Typeset by Dorchester Typesetting Group Ltd
Printed in Singapore by Tien Wah Press

1 3 5 7 9 10 8 6 4 2

www.glitterwingsacademy.co.uk

*To the memory of my
grandmother, Esther Cruce.
She always made Christmas magical.*

Chapter One

Twink Flutterby sat on the roof of her parents' cosy woodland stump and sighed happily. Her home was the best place in the world to spend the winter holidays! Especially when her best friend, Bimi Bluebell, was there as well. The two fairies smiled at each other.

'It's so beautiful here!' exclaimed Bimi. Looking around her, Twink had to agree. The fields and nearby woods all sparkled with frost, as if they were coated with diamond dust.

Already the two girls had packed a month's worth

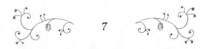

of fun into the week they'd been at Twink's: skating on the frozen brook with Teena, Twink's younger sister; making elaborate snow-fairies; sitting up late to hear Twink's parents tell stories – and eating lots of delicious honey cake!

'You know, it's funny,' said Twink thoughtfully. 'It's been such great hols, but I'm really missing Glitterwings.' The giant oak tree that housed Glitterwings Academy felt like home now.

'Me too,' said Bimi, nodding. 'But it won't be long before – oh!' She jumped up and rubbed her arm. 'Something hit me!'

Twink peered over the edge of the roof. 'Not some*thing* – some*one*!' she said grimly. Down below, Teena was perched on Brownie, the Flutterby family's mouse. Her arm was just stretched back to throw another snowball.

'Teena, stop that!' ordered Twink.

Teena giggled. 'Why should I? It's not fair for you two to fly up there where I can't follow.' Twink's little sister wouldn't learn to fly until she started her first term at Glitterwings in the spring – a fact that

caused her a great deal of frustration!

'Yes, that's the idea!' said Twink. She loved her little sister, but didn't want Teena tagging along after her and Bimi *all* the time.

'Oh! You mean thing!' screeched Teena.

Twink ducked as another snowball whizzed through the air. 'All right, you asked for it!' she laughed. 'Come on, Bimi, let's get her.'

She jetted off the stump, Bimi close behind. With a startled squawk, Teena nudged Brownie into a gallop. Mouse and fairy scampered across the field, zigzagging this way and that.

'Can't catch me!' yelled Teena over her shoulder.

'Just watch us!' Twink shouted back. Her lavender wings blurred as she darted around frozen blades of grass. 'Bimi, head her off!'

'With pleasure!' grinned Bimi.

Putting on a burst of speed, Bimi shot ahead, circling in front of Brownie. Teena gave a yelp and whirled the mouse the other way – but Twink was waiting for her! Swooping close, Twink grabbed Brownie's reins and tugged hard. He trotted to a stop.

'Ha! Got you!' cried Twink, pulling her sister off the mouse. 'Now, I think *someone* deserves a tickle attack. Don't you, Bimi?'

'Definitely!' said Bimi with a wicked smile. Her blue hair was tousled from the frenzied flight.

'No!' squealed Teena, shrieking with laughter. 'Let me go!' She fluttered her wings wildly as the older girls tickled her.

'Girls!' came Mum's voice from the tree stump. 'Would you like some hot nectar?'

Still laughing, the three fairies disentangled

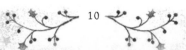

themselves and headed back to the stump. Twink and Bimi got there first, with Teena riding up on Brownie a moment later, her eyes shining with merriment.

They took the hot drinks gratefully, warming their hands around the acorn-shell cups. Twink sniffed hers with her eyes closed. Mmm! Nothing was nicer than hot nectar in the wintertime.

'Mum, what's that?' said Teena suddenly, pointing towards the woods.

Turning, Twink caught her breath. There was a human walking into the woods! But what was he carrying? Whatever it was, it glinted sharply in the winter sunshine.

Mum looked troubled. 'Oh dear! Your father won't be very pleased – they usually go to the other side of the forest. Oh, the poor trees!'

'What's wrong, Mrs Flutterby?' asked Bimi, her blue eyes wide.

'It always happens at this time of year,' explained Mum sadly. 'When the weather turns cold, humans start going into the woods and chopping down trees

– young, healthy evergreens! And then they carry the trees away with them.'

The three girls stared at her in horror. 'They – they chop down *trees*?' said Teena faintly.

Twink's little sister looked pale. Twink didn't blame her – she felt pretty pale herself. It was a fairy's duty to take care of nature. The thought of young trees being killed was awful!

'But *why*, Mrs Flutterby?' asked Bimi anxiously. 'What do they do with them?'

Mum shook her bright pink head. 'No one knows,' she said. 'Maybe they resent nature and want to hurt it. They're odd creatures, you know. Why, most of them don't even set foot in the woods except to cut down a tree once a year!'

Twink stared at the forest. Her heart was thudding so hard that it echoed in her ears. 'But we have to stop him!' she burst out. 'We can't just let him kill a tree for no reason!'

'I'm afraid there's nothing we can do,' said Mum. 'It's too dangerous for us to try tackling a human on our own, even with our magic. You never know what they might do!'

'But –' Twink choked to a halt as hot tears pricked her eyes.

Mum's voice turned brisk. 'I'm sorry, Twink. I don't like it either, but we fairies can't right every wrong, much as we might like to! Now, you girls go and play, and try to forget about this.'

Taking their empty acorn shells with her, Mum flitted back inside, and they heard her bustling about in the kitchen. The three fairies stayed where they were, not moving. Teena's violet eyes were huge.

'Twink, we *can't* just forget about it!' she whispered urgently. 'You and Bimi have got to do something!'

Twink bit her lip as she and Bimi glanced at each other. Do something? But what?

Suddenly a harsh noise rang through the air, like the distant cracking of a whip. The fairies froze. The sound came again – and again.

'Oh!' sobbed Teena. 'He's doing it! He's chopping down a tree!'

Twink's wings were trembling with fear and fury. She *couldn't* just stand here and let this happen!

'Bimi, come on,' she hissed, grabbing her friend's hand. 'Teena's right – we have to stop him!'

Bimi looked alarmed. 'But – humans are so big! What can *we* do?'

'I don't know, but we have to try!' insisted Twink. Without waiting for an answer, she flew off across the field, the cold wind whistling through her wings. For a moment she thought Bimi wouldn't follow, but then her friend came skimming after her.

Plunging into the woods, Twink darted through the trees, following the sound of chopping. Oh, they were going to be too late!

'Hurry, Bimi!' she shouted over her shoulder.

The noise of the axe grew louder and louder. Bursting out into a clearing, Twink saw a man in a red jacket standing beside a young spruce tree. The tree sagged sadly to one side, its trunk splintered and bitten. The axe gleamed as the man started to bring it down again.

'No!' screamed Twink. With Bimi just behind her,

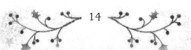

she flew straight at the man's face. 'Stop! Leave the tree alone!'

The man gave a surprised yelp and leapt back. 'What on –'

A sudden rush of courage seemed to fill Bimi. 'Go away!' she yelled, buzzing about his head in a blue and silver blur. 'We don't want you here!'

The man backed away, staring at Twink and Bimi with bulging eyes. His mouth fell open, and he shut it again with a snap.

'Can't you hear us?' cried Twink, bobbing in front of him. 'Leave the tree alone! Go home!' What was wrong with the man? She knew most humans didn't know about fairies, but surely he'd believe what was right in front of him.

The man shook his head briskly. 'I'm imagining things,' he muttered, pushing his cap back. 'They're just moths, that's all. Strange, this time of year!'

'*Moths?*' echoed Bimi in disbelief. 'Of course we're not!'

But the man had already pulled his cap back into place and stepped forward again, raising the

axe. Its blade shone.

'*No!*' Twink dived towards the axe as it *swooshed* downwards. Flinging her arms around its handle, she frantically pulled and tugged. The axe didn't even slow down.

Crack!

The blade hit the trunk. The impact flung Twink off like a gnat, and she catapulted straight into the tree. Its branches burst past her in a prickly green explosion.

'Oh!' gasped Twink when she finally crashed to a halt. She was deep within the tree, with spiky branches every way she looked. Bruised and shaking, she started to take off to join Bimi again – but strain as she might, nothing happened.

Why weren't her wings working? Twisting around in a panic, Twink saw both wings beating furiously – but her rose-petal dress was caught on a branch! Twink grabbed at the pink material, yanking hard, and succeeded only in snagging it further.

Crack! The axe hit the trunk again.

'Aargh!' Twink shrieked as the tree shuddered side-

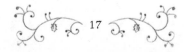

ways. Desperately, she gripped a nearby branch. She could hear Bimi screaming in the distance. Then the axe struck again and the tree fell, bouncing once on the ground.

Twink's eyes burned with tears. She bowed her cheek against the rough bark. That was that, then. The tree was dead, and nothing they could do now would save it. Oh, why hadn't the human listened to them? And why had he killed it? *Why*?

Suddenly the world heaved upwards. Peering through the dense branches, Twink saw the man's red jacket – and then the tree started to move. He was taking it away through the forest, with her in it!

Twink's wings went icy with terror as she remembered her mother's words: *And then they carry the trees away with them*. 'Stop!' she shouted, tugging at the branch that caught her. 'Oh, stop, stop!'

'Twink, where are you?' called Bimi's voice, squeaky with fear. 'Stop! You've got my best friend!'

The tree paused for a moment. 'Stupid moth!' growled the man, flapping his hand about his face. 'Get away from me, you daft thing.'

Twink heard Bimi cry out, and her pulse raced like a galloping horse. 'Leave Bimi alone!' she screamed. 'Don't you dare hurt her!'

The tree started moving again. Twink held back a sob. *Why* couldn't she get free? She seized her dress with both hands, wrenching and twisting. All at once the petal fabric ripped, and Twink felt herself come loose. Finally!

She started to jet out of the branches – and then screamed again, clutching at spruce needles as the tree shot up into the air. Twink's stomach lurched as she was flung wildly from side to side; then the tree seemed to slide and bounce . . . and stopped.

There was a slamming noise. Struggling free of the tree at last, Twink emerged from its branches – and stopped, hovering in bewilderment. Where *was* she? She was in a sort of large box with windows, with giant human-sized seats in it! The tree lay on its side, while the man sat with his back to her, fiddling with some sort of instrument.

'A car,' whispered Twink, remembering stories she had heard.

Cold dread gripped her. Cars were notorious among fairies: they were huge, smoking monsters, to be avoided at all costs. And now she was *in* one – and even worse, she was with this mad human! Twink looked fearfully at the back of the man's head, remembering how he had swiped at Bimi. She had to get out of here!

She darted from window to window, searching for a way out – but there was none; the massive panes of glass were as smooth and unyielding as glaciers. Then she saw Bimi skimming up outside the car. To Twink's immense relief, she didn't look hurt.

'Bimi!' she called, beating on a window with her fists. 'Bimi, I'm in here!'

The blue-haired fairy's eyes widened as she spotted Twink. She flitted up to the window, yelling something Twink couldn't hear.

'I can't get out!' cried Twink. 'Bimi, go and get my mum! Hurry, hurry!'

A roaring sound exploded through the car. Twink gasped, flinging her hands over her ears. The trees outside began to glide smoothly away.

The car was leaving!

'Bimi!' yelped Twink. 'Get my mum!'

Bimi didn't seem to hear. She sped after the car, her silver and gold wings a blur, but it very soon became too fast for her. Twink watched her best friend grow smaller and smaller as the car picked up speed . . . until finally she lost sight of her altogether.

No! No! Twink's heart pounded in her chest. She stared out of the window for a long time, unable to believe what had happened. When the view outside

became one of other cars and long, unending roads, Twink shivered and flew away from the window, curling up beside the tree.

'We're both trapped,' she whispered, stroking the tree's rough bark with a trembling hand. 'Where is he taking us?'

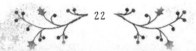

Chapter Two

The car travelled for what seemed a very long time, until Twink felt quite ill with the unnatural motion. Hugging herself, she closed her eyes and moaned. How on earth did humans do this all the time? They must have stomachs made of steel!

Finally, just when Twink's wings were drooping with distress and she thought she couldn't bear it any longer, the car slowed . . . and stopped.

Twink opened her eyes cautiously. They had really stopped moving! Skimming up to the window again, she gazed out eagerly, hoping to see

she recognised.

car had stopped on a human street. They
re surrounded by rows and rows of human
houses. Twink stared in horror. There were no trees
anywhere! No fields, no frozen streams! She couldn't
even see a blade of grass.

A gust of cold air swirled into the car as the man
opened his door. Twink sped towards the opening –
and then jumped backwards with a yelp as the heavy
door slammed shut. What now? She looked around
her in despair.

Suddenly the whole back of the car opened up,
and the man's face loomed in! Twink darted back
into the tree to hide, wincing at the rough prickles.

She clung to the tree's branches as it was dragged
from the car. With a start, Twink saw the man's
hand appear just beside her, grasping the trunk. She
stared at it in horrified fascination. It looked like a
giant spider!

The tree bounced and shook as the man carried it.
The motion stopped, and there was a ringing
sound. Twink cringed as a dog barked nearby.

Thank goodness she was hidden! Then she heard a door opening.

'Merry Christmas!' boomed the man. He gave the tree a shake. 'Was it worth taking the afternoon off?'

'Tom, it's beautiful!' exclaimed a woman's voice. 'Lindsay's going to be thrilled!'

The tree started moving again. Peering out through the spiky branches, Twink saw in alarm that she was being carried into the human's house! The dog – a portly-looking thing with black fur – sniffed at the tree and then leapt back, barking sharply.

It can smell me! realised Twink, her wings clammy with dread. Though fairies were the caretakers of nature, most dogs didn't seem to grasp this. They saw fairies as they would any small, exciting creature, and loved to chase them when they could.

'Oh, hush, Clarence! Go to your bed,' scolded the woman's voice. 'I've got the stand all ready,' she continued. 'Let's put it here!'

Twink held back a shriek as the tree was swung upright again, back into its natural position. But there was nothing natural about what she could glimpse now through the branches. The humans were attaching the tree to some sort of base, so that it stood up straight. Then the woman fetched a large watering can and watered it!

Twink gaped in bewilderment. *What* was going on? Mum had said that humans were odd creatures – but this was odder than anything Twink could have imagined!

'Lovely!' cried the woman. 'I'll go and get the lights. But we'll let Lindsay decorate it when she gets home from school – it'll be a nice start to her Christmas holiday.'

'Of course, that's her job!' said the man cheerfully. His voice grew more distant. 'I'll put the kettle on, shall I?'

Cautiously, Twink edged her way towards the outer branches of the tree and peeked out. She was in a human living room, with giant-sized chairs and a carpet of unnatural grey that looked the size of a field.

Twink stared. There were so many *things*! There

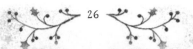

was a large box in the corner with black cords snaking out from it; tables with brightly burning lamps; shelves filled with shiny, square objects. How did humans *breathe* with so much around them?

The dog lay curled up in a bed beside the fireplace. At the sight of Twink he lunged to his feet, barking. She had to hide! Twink shot across the room to the window, diving between the curtain's folds.

'WOOF! WOOF! *WOOF-WOOF-WOOF-WOOF-WOOF!*'

The dog bounded after her, yapping hysterically. Trembling, Twink hovered deep within the darkness of the curtains. Any moment now the dog's jaws might tear the material down and snatch her up!

'*Clarence!*' snapped the woman's voice. 'WHAT are you barking at?'

The dog's barks turned to an urgent whine. The woman strode briskly across the carpet, dragging Clarence away.

'Silly old thing! I suppose the ginger cat's been making faces at you through the window again.

Well, you'll just have to stay in your bed until you calm down!'

There was a snorting noise as the dog let out a frustrated breath. Then silence fell. Twink risked a look from between the curtain's folds, and her eyes widened. The woman was busy wrapping a thin green rope around the tree. *What* was she doing?

As Twink watched, the woman started humming happily to herself. 'Oh, don't you love Christmas, Clarence?' she said.

Stepping back, the woman inspected her work with satisfaction. 'And look, this is the best part.' Bending down, she did something to the rope – and suddenly the tree exploded into light!

Twink gasped. Oh, it was so pretty! Like hundreds of sparkling icicles, all winking and glittering at once.

'Perfect,' said the woman, turning the lights off. Twink let out a disappointed breath as they vanished. 'We'll do the rest when Lindsay gets home, right, Clarence?'

Clarence was lying in his bed with his nose

propped on his paws, staring dismally at Twink. He whined when the woman spoke to him, but she didn't seem to notice. She had taken out a circular white cloth and was arranging it prettily under the tree.

Twink made up her mind all at once. Though the man was quite clearly mad – convinced that Twink was a *moth*, of all things! – his wife seemed much more sensible. Surely *she* would believe her own eyes, and want to help a poor stranded fairy?

Flying out into the room, Twink hovered near the woman's shoulder, waving a hand to catch her attention. 'Hello!' she called. 'Can you see me?'

Brushing off her hands, the woman hopped to her feet. 'There! Now, I wonder where Tom's got to with that tea, eh, Clarence? Drunk it all himself, I expect!'

'Um . . . hello?' The woman started to turn away, and Twink darted after her, bobbing directly in front of her face. 'Wait – I need your help!'

'Oh!' The woman stopped short. Her eyes went perfectly round as human and fairy gazed at each

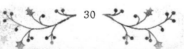

other. Twink let out a relieved breath. At last! Now all she had to do was ask for help.

'Hi, I'm Twink!' she said with a friendly smile. 'There's been a – well, a sort of mix-up, I suppose. You see –'

'AARGH!' screeched the woman, stumbling backwards.

A door banged open, and the man rushed into the room. 'What's wrong?' he shouted.

'It talked! It talked!' cried the woman, pointing at Twink. The dog leapt to its feet, barking wildly.

Twink had flown off the moment the woman screamed. She darted around the room in a panic, unable to find a hiding place where they wouldn't spot her. Oh, *why* had she tried to speak to another human? She was such a moss brain!

'It's the moth,' she heard the man bellow. 'I don't believe it – it followed me home from the woods!'

'It's not a moth! It *talked*!' insisted the woman. 'It – *oh*!' she jumped sideways as Twink swooped near her. The dog yipped and yelped, bouncing about on its hind legs.

'Don't be silly, it couldn't have!' The man made a grab for Twink as she zoomed past. She shrieked. She could feel the breeze from his hand!

Panting hard, Twink flew up to a cluster of lights that hung from the ceiling. They were fire-hot, but she was too frantic to care. She crouched behind one, making herself as small as possible.

'It *is* a moth, I tell you,' continued the man. Twink gulped as she saw him scowling up at her. 'There were two of them – they flew right in my face and made a horrible squeaking noise! It happened in the woods as I was chopping down the tree.'

'A horrible squeaking – yes, that's just what happened to me!' gasped his wife. Pressing her hands to her forehead, she gave a shaky laugh. 'Oh, Tom, is it *really* a moth? I thought I had gone completely doolally!'

The man nodded. 'It gave me quite a start at first, too – must be some sort of optical illusion. But it's only a moth. Come and see for yourself!'

The woman joined him, and the two humans

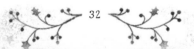

stared up at Twink as she perched in the chandelier. She gazed back warily. Her wings felt like sizzling leaves, but she wasn't about to move. There was no telling what such a pair of lunatics might do!

'Yes, you're right – it *is* a moth,' said the woman in relief. 'How could I have ever thought . . . well, never mind! Its wings are rather pretty, aren't they?'

'Pink and lavender – very girly,' laughed her husband. 'We'll have to show it to Lindsay.'

The woman shook her head. 'No, she hates big flapping insects! Tom, catch it, won't you? We'll chuck it outside before she gets home.'

Yes! Twink's spirits shot up like a fountain – but then she froze in horror at the man's next words.

'You and your soft heart!' he scoffed affectionately. 'You don't *catch* moths, love – you swat them.' He picked up what looked like the human version of a petal mag, rolling it into a tight cylinder.

Twink's heart flipped over in her chest. *Swat them?* He couldn't mean –

Wooosh! The magazine missed Twink by a wing's

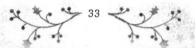

breadth as it came whistling down. The chandelier swung wildly.

'Aargh!' screamed Twink. She dived off, flying as fast as she could. But *where*? There was no place to hide! Holding back a terrified sob, she flew dizzily about the room, with the magazine crashing and thrashing after her.

'Stay *still*,' ordered the man. Twink put on another burst of speed. He had to be joking!

'Oh, I can't watch!' cried his wife. 'I'm going upstairs.'

She opened a door Twink hadn't noticed before and rushed out. There! As the door started to shut again, Twink winged after her, doing a quick barrel roll to twist through the narrow opening just before it shut in her face.

She was in a corridor, with the closed front door at the end of it. Twink hovered for a moment, wondering if she should try to get through it – and then the door she had just come through was flung open.

'Ah-ha – there you are!' said the man, waving the magazine.

Chapter Three

With a shriek, Twink shot past him in the other direction – up a flight of stairs, those strange things used by humans to climb from floor to floor. The woman was already halfway up them, and Twink darted around her as she flew upwards. There was a startled squeal.

'Tom! It's up here!'

'I know!' Twink could hear the man's heavy footsteps pounding after her. Gasping with terror, she skimmed down the upstairs corridor and ducked into the first open room she saw.

She had a quick, shadowy impression of pink and white. Glancing around frantically, Twink spotted a small house on the floor, with one wall missing. There was no time to wonder about it. She jetted to the little house and landed inside.

There was actually *furniture* in here, just Twink's size! She huddled behind an armchair, folding her wings tightly against her back.

Just then the two humans came rushing in. There was a *click*, and light flooded down from the ceiling. Twink swallowed hard. *Oh, please don't let them see me!*

'Oh no – where has it gone?' moaned the woman. 'If it starts flapping around in here tonight, Lindsay will have nightmares for a week!'

'Don't worry, we'll catch it,' said her husband. 'It'll start flying around the light in a moment – moths always do.'

Not this *moth,* thought Twink grimly, not moving a muscle. Her heart was thudding so loudly that she was sure the humans would hear it – but the minutes passed, and nothing happened. She listened as the man rustled the curtains, trying to scare the 'moth' out.

'Oh, I give up,' he said finally. 'We'll just have to wait for it to come out on its own – wretched thing.'

'Look at the time!' exclaimed his wife. 'I've got to collect Lindsay.'

Twink slumped as the room fell into shadow again. The two humans departed, closing the door behind them. Their voices faded away down the corridor.

Slowly, Twink edged out from behind the tiny

chair. She felt bruised and shaken from the long day – and also very thirsty, now that she had a moment to catch her breath. But there was no way to get any water.

Sinking on to the floor of the tiny house, Twink thought longingly of her parents. They were probably searching for her right now, their hearts breaking with fear and worry. Oh, *why* hadn't she listened to her mum? She'd been an idiot to think she and Bimi could take on a human by themselves!

Tears pricked at Twink's eyes. If she could only get out of this mess, she'd never behave rashly again, not ever. But how could she get away when she was too terrified even to move? That man was ready to swat her flat the moment he saw her!

Twink gave in to her frightened tears, hugging her knees to her chest as she sobbed. After a while she wiped her eyes wearily. *I've got to think of a plan*, she thought. *Crying's no good. Sooze wouldn't cry, nor would Pix.*

The thought of her friends gave her courage. Why, even Bimi probably wouldn't cry! Though perhaps not as bold or as conspicuously clever as Sooze or Pix, Twink's best friend had loads of common sense. She would most likely have worked out exactly what to do by now.

I will too, Twink promised herself, holding back a yawn. She knew she had to think of a plan, but the long, awful day had finally caught up with her. She felt as if she'd never been so tired in her life.

It's only for a few minutes, thought Twink drowsily as she curled up on the floor of the tiny house. *I'll work out what to do just as soon as I have a little rest . . .*

And in no time at all Twink was snoring softly, her lavender wings folded around her like a blanket.

Some time later Twink stirred, fluttering her wings with a yawn. Oh, what an awful dream she'd had! That poor tree – and herself, trapped in a human house! She could hardly wait to tell Bimi and Teena about it; they'd be agog.

But . . . why was her bed so hard? And what was that strange, harsh light?

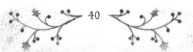

Suddenly Twink sat bolt upright. It hadn't been a dream at all! Here she was, in the tiny house – and –

'Oh!' Twink stifled a shriek, her hands flying to her mouth.

Looming in front of her like a giant moon was the face of a human child. She had long blonde hair and a spray of freckles across her nose, and was staring at Twink as if she couldn't believe her eyes.

For a long moment Twink and the child looked at each other. Twink's heart was hammering like a woodpecker. She opened her mouth to say something, and then hastily closed it. She wasn't about to try *that* again!

But the girl spoke first. 'Are you real?' she whispered. Her voice was hushed and respectful.

'Of course!' burst out Twink in surprise.

Very gently, the little girl touched Twink's wing with a finger almost as tall as Twink. 'Oh, I *knew* there were really fairies!' she breathed, her eyes shining. 'I told Sarah so, but she didn't believe me.'

Relief swept over Twink like sudden sunshine on a cloudy day. 'You know I'm a fairy, then?' she cried.

Her wings fluttered so hard that she shot up into the air. 'You can really see me?'

'You can fly!' squealed the little girl. 'But don't do it in there, or you'll hit your head,' she added anxiously.

Twink saw what she meant – the ceiling was alarmingly low. Leaving the tiny house, she flew out into the room, which she saw now must belong to the girl. The furniture was all white and shining, and the bedcover had a pattern of pink daisies.

The little girl scrambled to her feet. She was wearing a pair of blue leg-coverings, and a bright pink top. She had nice eyes, decided Twink. Not quite green and not quite brown, but a pleasant woodland shade that was somewhere in between.

'Are you Lindsay?' she asked, remembering the name she'd heard earlier.

The girl's eyes grew even rounder. 'How did you know? Is it – is it magic?'

Twink grinned. 'No, sorry! I heard your parents say it. I'm Twink,' she offered, hovering in front of Lindsay and extending her hand.

'Hello, Twink. I'm pleased to meet you,' said Lindsay. She touched a careful finger to Twink's hand, and the two girls suddenly found themselves giggling. It was like a mountain trying to shake hands with an ant!

Why, humans could be as friendly as fairies. Twink's wings warmed at the thought. 'I'm pleased to meet you, too,' she said earnestly. 'Only – only – I'm not really pleased to be here! You see, I've got trapped.'

'Trapped?' echoed Lindsay. 'What happened?' She sat cross-legged on her bed.

Twink hesitated, uncertain what was polite when you were a fairy talking to a human. But her wings were getting tired, so she swooped down to land on one of Lindsay's blue-clad knees.

The faded fabric was surprisingly comfortable. She leaned back on her hands to tell her tale. 'Well, my best friend has been visiting me for the winter holidays, you see, and this morning . . .'

Lindsay turned out to be a very good listener. Her expression showed she was taking in every word, but

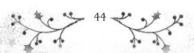

she sat quietly while Twink spoke, only occasionally breathing an 'Oh no!' or 'How awful!'

But when Twink described what happened once she got into the house, Lindsay gasped in horror. 'Oh, Twink, I'm sorry!' she burst out. 'My dad didn't mean any harm – he'd never have hurt you if he'd known you're a fairy! He just doesn't like insects very much, especially in the house.'

Twink made a face. She didn't want to insult Lindsay's father, but even swatting a moth seemed pretty terrible to her. They were such harmless creatures! What had a moth ever done to *him*?

But it didn't seem a very tactful subject, so Twink took a deep breath and finished her story.

'Anyway, then I hid in that little house, and they couldn't find me – but *you* did! I wonder why you can see me and your parents can't?' she added with a puzzled frown.

'Well, they *can* see you,' said Lindsay. 'They just think you're a moth.'

Twink shook her head. 'But they both saw me at first – I mean *really* saw me, I'm sure of it. And they

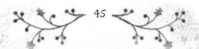

45

heard me, too, but then they told themselves they hadn't. It doesn't make any sense.'

'I know,' nodded Lindsay. 'Grown-ups are funny sometimes. Most of them don't believe in magic, or – or fairies, or ghosts, or *anything* interesting. In fact . . .' she faltered, her cheeks growing red.

'What?' asked Twink.

Lindsay hunched her shoulders sheepishly. 'Well, a lot of kids don't either. But *I* do. I always have, and see – I'm right!' She grinned, and Twink smiled back.

'I just don't understand one thing, though,' said Lindsay, carefully changing position with Twink still on her knee. 'Why were you so upset about the tree?'

'*Why?*' Twink gaped at her, almost spluttering in her astonishment. 'Because – because it's a living thing!'

'But it's only a tree,' said Lindsay blankly. 'It's not like chopping down a *person*. Besides, there's loads more of them. It came from Uncle Matt's farm, and he's got thousands!'

Twink's wings shivered in indignation. But

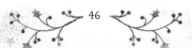

Lindsay was a human, she reminded herself – and even very nice humans obviously didn't understand these things.

'Well, we fairies think differently about it,' she said. 'We know the trees really well. They all have different personalities, and lots of them have dryads living inside them, and –'

'What's a dryad?' broke in Lindsay.

Twink floundered. How could anyone not know what a *dryad* was? 'It's a – well, like a nature spirit,' she said. 'They live inside trees – they're part of them.'

'Really?' cried Lindsay. Then the girl's face paled abruptly. 'Oh! There wasn't one living in *our* tree, was there?'

'I don't think so,' said Twink sadly. 'I hope not.'

Lindsay was silent for a moment, biting her lip. 'I'm sorry,' she said finally. 'I suppose I understand a little better now. It's just that Christmas trees are so pretty, and Mum always says you have to have a real one for the smell . . .'

Twink blinked in confusion. 'A Christmas tree?

But it was a baby spruce your dad cut down.'

'Yes, but it's a Christmas tree, too,' said Lindsay eagerly. 'Oh, Twink, you should see it now! We spent all afternoon decorating it.'

'But what *is* a Christmas tree?' asked Twink.

'Don't you know?' exclaimed Lindsay, bouncing on to her knees. Twink quickly took to the air, hovering in front of her. 'They're the most magical, wonderful things in the world!'

Twink listened in amazement as Lindsay launched

into an explanation that included something called a manger, and the birth of a baby, and presents and fairy lights.

'*Fairy* lights?' she repeated.

Lindsay's blonde hair tumbled about her face as she nodded. 'Yes, that's what they're called! 'Cos they sparkle like little fairies.'

Except that fairies don't sparkle, thought Twink dazedly.

She was sitting cross-legged on Lindsay's bedside table by then, beside a stuffed ladybird that was taller than she was. She stared into its blank eyes and shivered. Oh, she wanted to go home! She liked Lindsay, but this was all much too confusing and strange.

'Lindsay, would you help me?' she asked. She flitted to the girl's knee again, looking up at her earnestly. 'I need to fly home, only I don't know where it is from here. Could you point me in the right direction?'

Lindsay's face fell. 'Oh! Do you really have to go so soon?'

Twink nodded. 'I really, really do. My parents must be frantic by now. They don't even know where I am!' The thought of it brought a hard lump to her throat.

Concern creased the girl's face. 'You're right,' she said. '*My* parents would go out of their minds if I went missing! You've got to get home – only . . .' Lindsay trailed off, frowning.

'What?' cried Twink.

Lindsay shrugged. 'Well . . . I don't know where it is.'

Chapter Four

'*You don't?*' echoed Twink. 'But I thought –'

Lindsay shook her head. 'Uncle Matt's not really my uncle; he's a friend of Dad's. I've only been to his farm once, to help Dad – well, you-know-what,' she said awkwardly. 'But that was *years* ago.'

'Don't you have *any* idea where it is?' asked Twink desperately.

Lindsay bit her lip. 'Um . . . not really. But my dad knows!' she said, brightening. 'I'll ask him tonight. Don't worry, Twink. You'll be home soon, I promise!'

Later, after Lindsay had gone downstairs to eat, Twink hovered at the window and stared out at the strange world of the humans. How she longed for the sight of a friendly wood or a tinkling stream! But there was none – just street after street of brightly lit houses, gleaming in the winter darkness.

Many of the houses had sparkling trees in their windows, and Twink gazed at them in confusion. Mum was wrong, she thought. Humans didn't cut down trees because they hated nature at all. There was a lot more to it than that – though exactly what, Twink still wasn't sure!

Lost in thought, she flitted back to the bedside table. Lindsay had brought her some water in a tiny teacup from her doll's house, but it was still the size of a bucket to Twink. Straining, she managed to pick it up and took a few sips.

Urgh! She made a face and hastily put it down again. Give her fresh dew any day!

Lindsay had also left her a piece of something called 'chocolate'. The thick brown square squatted

on the table and Twink looked at it doubtfully. Was *this* what humans ate? Something that resembled a slab of dried mud?

Hunger rumbled in Twink's stomach. Breaking off a tiny piece of the chocolate, she gave it a cautious sniff before putting it in her mouth.

Oh! Twink's eyes widened as the most amazing taste flowed through her – rich and sweet and thoroughly delicious. Settling down beside the brown square, she happily ate her fill, licking her fingers to get every last bit.

When she'd finished, Twink glanced at the bedroom door. Had Lindsay spoken to her father yet? With any luck, Twink would be able to set off from Lindsay's bedroom window that very night! She grinned as she imagined her parents' faces when she came swooping back into the tree stump. What a story she'd have to tell!

Tapping her wings together idly, Twink's mind drifted back to the Christmas tree. *What* made the humans do such a strange thing? Still, she had to admit the tree had looked very pretty with the fairy lights sparkling on it. And Lindsay had said it was 'decorated' now. What did *that* mean?

Twink looked at the door again, curiosity tugging at her. It seemed a shame not to find out more about the Christmas tree while she could. What if she were the first fairy ever to go inside a human house? She *had* to find out more; this might be the only chance any fairy would get!

The thought decided her, despite the danger. Squaring her shoulders, Twink skimmed across the room. The door was slightly ajar. She slipped through, and flew down the darkened stairs.

Hovering outside the door at the bottom, she peered through the glass. Lindsay and her parents were sitting around a table, eating dinner and talking. Clarence the dog sat expectantly beside Lindsay, his head following every movement of her fork.

Good – if she were careful, none of them would notice her. Twink inspected the door. It was firmly closed, but now that she wasn't in such a panic, she could see there was a good-sized gap at the bottom.

A moment later she had squeezed through and was in the dining area. The Christmas tree was at the opposite end of the room, where the sofas were.

'Yes, and that's not all,' Lindsay's mother was saying. 'You won't believe what he told me next –'

Twink didn't wait to hear. Ducking behind a sofa, she half ran, half flew down the length of the long room. When she darted out into the open, she gasped.

Before, the tree had only had lights on it. Now its branches were adorned with bright, dangling figures and gleaming glass baubles. Ropes of bristling silver

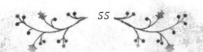

were draped about the tree like necklaces, and right at its very top sat a shining star.

Twink flew slowly around the sparkling tree, taking in every detail. She had never seen anything so beautiful! Suddenly she stopped, her eyes widening. One of the dangling figures was a fairy, with holly-leaf wings and a white dress garlanded with ivy.

Twink flitted to the decoration and stared into its face. It really *was* a fairy! Her painted features smiled at Twink.

'Dad, where's Uncle Matt's farm?' came Lindsay's voice from across the room.

This was it! Twink landed on a branch beside the little fairy, her pointed ears craning to catch every word.

'Up near Wenton,' said Lindsay's father. 'Why?'

'Just wondering,' said Lindsay. She slipped a bit of food to Clarence, who wolfed it down. 'Er . . . what direction is that in?'

Lindsay's mother laughed. 'You must be doing geography in school.'

57

'That's right.' Lindsay nodded vigorously. 'So which direction is it, Dad?'

'From here, you mean?' Lindsay's father considered. 'North-east, I suppose.'

'Which way's that? Can you show me?'

With an eyebrow-raised glance at Lindsay's mother, her father twisted in his seat and pointed towards the front of the house. 'That way, roughly. That do you?'

'Yes, thanks, Dad! That's brilliant.' Lindsay's freckled face beamed.

Ask how far it is! implored Twink silently as she perched on the prickly branch. *I need to know how far!*

Miraculously, Lindsay seemed to hear. 'Dad . . . how long does it take to get there?'

'About an hour, motorway willing,' said Lindsay's father. 'Why all the questions, Lin? Are you planning on going there?'

Twink clutched the branch excitedly. Of course she knew that cars went faster than fairies, but surely if a car took an hour to make the journey, then she could fly it in three or four? She'd be home before morning!

But Lindsay didn't look so sure. She bit her lip. 'Um . . . how far away is that in miles?'

Her father put down his fork with a groan. 'It's about fifty miles away. Now, do you need anything else? The postcode, perhaps? Grid reference on an Ordnance Survey map?'

'Tom, she's only asking,' chided Lindsay's mother.

All the blood seemed to rush from Twink's head, leaving her faint and dizzy. *Fifty miles?* That was further than the strongest fairy in the world could fly!

Lindsay's face had paled. 'Fifty miles? But . . .'

'*What?*' said her father in exasperation.

'Nothing.' Lindsay looked down, her fork scraping as she toyed with her food. Suddenly she glanced up again, her face full of hope. 'Dad! Could you take me there?'

Of course! Twink held her breath as she saw Lindsay's plan. If Lindsay's father would drive her there, then Twink could sneak along! She'd be home in no time.

'What for?' Lindsay's father gazed at her as though she had lost her senses.

'Sweetie, what's up?' put in Lindsay's mum. 'Why all this interest in Uncle Matt's farm all of a sudden?'

'Because . . . because . . .' Lindsay's cheeks turned pink as she floundered.

Twink froze in terror. *Don't tell them!* she shouted silently. She trusted Lindsay, but she didn't trust Lindsay's parents one little bit! They'd come after her with the rolled-up magazine again.

'Because I want to see where you chopped down

the tree!' burst out Lindsay finally. Twink's wings sagged in relief.

Her parents stared at her. 'Why would you want to see that?' asked her father.

'I – I want to say sorry to it.' Lindsay's cheeks were on fire, but she lifted her chin firmly. 'For being chopped down.'

'You want to say sorry to the tree stump,' repeated her father in disbelief. 'Now I've heard everything!'

'It must be something she heard in school,' put in Lindsay's mother. 'Darling, why are you so worried about the tree? We cut one down every year! You always say how pretty it is.'

Lindsay looked near tears. 'Because it was a living thing! Trees have personalities, and lots of them have dryads, and –'

'*Dryads?*' Her father burst out laughing. 'You've been reading too many fairytales! The tree didn't have a dryad, I promise.'

How would you *know?* thought Twink. Her wings quivered with anger. He probably didn't even believe in dryads, much less care if he chopped one down!

'It *might* have,' insisted Lindsay. 'Dad, will you take me there? Please?'

'So you can say sorry to a tree stump? No, I don't think so! You can say sorry to the Christmas tree, if you must. Coffee, Karen?' Pushing back his chair, he stomped off towards the kitchen. Clarence followed, wagging his tail.

'Lindsay, I think you've upset Dad,' whispered Lindsay's mother. 'You know how much he loves bringing the tree home to us every year.'

'I know, but . . .' Lindsay hesitated. 'Mum, could *you* take me? Please? It's really important!'

Her mother grimaced. 'Oh, Lindsay! Maybe later, after the holidays.'

'*When* after the holidays?' pressed Lindsay.

'I don't know! Sometime. Now just leave it, all right?' Rising from the table, Lindsay's mother started stacking the dishes.

Glumly, Lindsay got to her feet. 'May I please be excused?'

Her mother paused. 'Don't you want dessert? It's apple pie.'

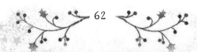

'No, thank you,' said Lindsay. 'I think I'll just go up to my room now.'

'Suit yourself!' sighed Lindsay's mother, disappearing into the kitchen.

Twink shot out from the tree, leaving the fairy decoration trembling behind her. As Lindsay left the room, she put on a burst of speed, flitting through the door just before it closed. Lindsay saw her, and gasped.

'Twink! What are *you* doing here?' She popped a hand over her mouth, looking over her shoulder. But no sound came from her parents. 'Come on!' she hissed, and she galloped up the stairs with Twink flying right behind her.

'I heard everything,' admitted Twink once they were safely back in Lindsay's room. Her heart was thudding as she touched down on Lindsay's bedside table. 'Oh, Lindsay! Fifty miles – what am I going to do? It's hopeless!'

Chapter Five

'There *must* be a way,' said Lindsay. She bent down so that she could look Twink in the eyes. Her own were round and worried. 'Don't give up, Twink! You'll get home again.'

'*How?*' demanded Twink. 'Neither of your parents will drive you!'

'Well, maybe – maybe if you talked to them again, we could convince them you're a fairy! Then they'd be sure to want to help.' Lindsay's face lit up.

'No!' cried Twink, shooting up in the air. 'Lindsay, please – promise me you won't. Your parents will try

to swat me if they see me again!'

Lindsay didn't look completely convinced, but she nodded. 'All right, I promise. Don't worry, Twink, I won't say a word.'

Reassured, Twink drifted back down to the bedside table. 'What will we do, then?' she asked, rubbing her wings together anxiously. 'I've got to get home, Lindsay; I've just got to!'

Lindsay's forehead creased. 'Fairies must have to travel long distances *sometimes*,' she said. 'What do you do then?'

Twink considered. 'Well . . . we usually ride birds for any journey that's over a mile or two.'

'*Do* you?' breathed Lindsay, clearly enchanted by this information. 'Well, then, why can't you do that? My mum's got a bird feeder in the back garden; we get loads of birds every morning!'

Twink thought of Sunny, the faithful grey and yellow tit she had ridden in her first term at Glitterwings, and hope prickled through her. 'Oh, Lindsay, that might work!' she burst out.

'Great!' Lindsay jumped up. 'I'll set my alarm for

really early, and we'll sneak into the back garden before Mum and Dad wake up.' Then her face fell. 'Oh, why am I so excited?' she wailed. 'It just means you'll be leaving!'

Twink took quickly to the air, brushing a wing against Lindsay's cheek. 'Don't be sad,' she said warmly. 'I'll never forget you, Lindsay. I'll tell my family all about you!'

Lindsay managed a small smile. 'I won't forget you either, Twink. Not ever.'

That evening the two girls talked for ages, exchanging stories about their lives. Lindsay was open-mouthed when Twink described Glitterwings Academy: the spreading oak tree school on its hill, with tiny golden windows spiralling up its trunk and hundreds of fairy students swooping about inside.

'It's like something out of a story!' she said, hugging her knees. 'But why haven't humans ever found it?'

'I don't know,' admitted Twink. Now that she thought about it, she realised there must be some

66

sort of magic involved. Though, then again, if most humans were like Lindsay's parents, they'd just convince themselves that they'd seen a tree full of moths!

'Tell me more about Christmas trees,' she said. She was sitting perched on Lindsay's knee again, which now had the pink cotton of Lindsay's nightdress draped over it. 'I still don't understand, Lindsay. Why do humans have them?'

Lindsay's freckled face screwed up in thought. 'Well – not *all* humans do,' she said. 'But I think most people in this country do. And America. It's a – a tradition.'

'But what are they *for*?' Twink fluttered her wings despairingly.

'They're to celebrate Christmas,' explained Lindsay. 'It's a holiday, that's all. You sing special songs, and there's a big dinner, and you get *lots* of presents, though it's not really supposed to be about that, and –'

'But *how* does the tree celebrate Christmas?' broke in Twink. Special songs and presents sounded nice –

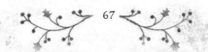

but they didn't have much to do with cutting down a baby spruce, so far as she could tell!

Suddenly the door to Lindsay's room flew open. 'Time for – oh!' Lindsay's mother started as she caught sight of Twink. 'It's that moth again! Lindsay, what's it doing on your *knee*?'

'It's – it's pretty,' said Lindsay weakly.

Lindsay's mother shook her head in amazement. 'But you're terrified of moths!'

'Not this one,' said Lindsay. 'It's my friend.'

'Your *friend*?' laughed Lindsay's mother. She came forward, holding her dressing gown around herself. Twink gulped, frozen in place. She felt as exposed as a frog on a log!

'It *is* pretty, isn't it?' said Lindsay's mother, staring down. Twink looked back at her uneasily, holding her wings very still. 'I wonder what it's doing out at this time of year?'

'Maybe it's lost its way,' said Lindsay softly. 'Maybe it wants to go home again.' Very gently, she reached out and stroked Twink's wing.

For a moment Lindsay's mother looked confused

as she gazed at Twink. Then she shook her head firmly. 'What an imagination! Promise me you'll put it out of the window before you go to bed, Lindsay; you know how your father feels about insects. Besides, you're right – it probably wants to go home again, poor thing.'

Twink went limp as Lindsay's mother left the room. 'That was close!' she whispered.

Lindsay nodded worriedly. 'We can't let her see you again or she *will* put you outside – and it's cold out there!'

That night Twink slept in the tiny house, which Lindsay said her grandfather had made for her. 'My friend Sarah says it's babyish,' she confessed, her cheeks reddening, 'but I still like playing with it.'

The little bed was just Twink's size, though it felt hard and strange until Lindsay tucked her up in something called a 'mitten'. 'Are you all right in there?' she asked, peering in at Twink.

'Perfect,' sighed Twink, nestling down into the soft red material. 'Goodnight, Lindsay – see you in the morning!'

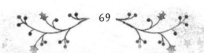

Twink thought she'd fall asleep immediately, but instead she lay awake for a long time, staring up at the doll's house ceiling. What a day it had been! She felt exhausted from all the emotions and new discoveries.

Most of all, she longed to be back with her family. They must be so worried about her by now! And poor Bimi – she probably thought it was all her fault for not stopping the human from taking Twink in the first place.

Don't worry, everyone, thought Twink. *I'll be home soon!*

Just before she drifted off, her thoughts wandered back to the Christmas tree sparkling downstairs. Who would have thought that humans would treat the trees they chopped down so lovingly, and decorate them so beautifully? Twink snuggled drowsily into the mitten. It was such a mystery . . . and the more Lindsay tried to explain, the more puzzling the whole thing became.

'You're still here!' hissed an excited voice.

'Oh!' Twink jolted awake as she saw Lindsay staring in at her, a huge grin on her face. Yawning, Twink crawled out of the mitten and stretched her wings. 'Of course I'm still here,' she said tetchily. 'I'm stuck, remember?'

Lindsay looked embarrassed. 'I know – I just thought maybe I'd dreamed you. Here, do you want some breakfast?' She offered Twink another bit of chocolate.

Wishing that she had a thistle comb to groom her long pink hair, Twink accepted, sitting on the doll's house floor to eat. Never mind – her hair wouldn't

stay tidy for long anyway if she was going to be riding a bird!

Twink's heart quickened at the thought. 'What time is it?' she asked, licking the last bit of chocolate from her fingers.

'Six o'clock,' said Lindsay, her eyes shining with excitement. 'It's still dark outside!'

A few minutes later Lindsay and Twink were sneaking down the stairs, Lindsay tiptoeing slowly while Twink flitted by her side. Lindsay eased open the downstairs door, and the two of them slipped into the lounge.

'Shh, Clarence. Be quiet!' whispered Lindsay as the black dog came trotting over. Twink stiffened as he caught sight of her. Oh no! He'd start barking and wake up Lindsay's parents!

But Lindsay grabbed Clarence by the collar and looked him in the eye. 'Twink is a *friend*,' she said sternly. 'Do you understand, Clarence? She's a *friend*, so you're not to bark at her!'

Fairy and dog stared doubtfully at each other. Twink put on a friendly smile. She thought the dog didn't seem at all convinced, but then the tip of his tail wagged.

'See, he likes you,' said Lindsay.

Twink grinned. Flitting forward, she stroked the dog's silky ear. 'Good dog,' she said – and then shrieked as he turned and licked her! 'Oh!' she gasped, gazing down at her rose-petal dress. She was drenched!

Lindsay burst into giggles. 'He *really* likes you!'

She took Twink into the kitchen, and ran something called a 'tap' for her so that Twink could wash in the warm water. Afterwards, Twink dried herself on a cloth that Lindsay said was used for dishes.

'The birds should be up by now,' said Twink. She could just see the first rays of the sun shining through the window.

Lindsay nodded. 'Come on!'

She led the way into what she called a 'conservatory'. Twink's heart lifted as she spotted the garden beyond. She'd been starting to think there was no greenery at all in Lindsay's world, but here it was: the rectangular space was filled with grass and flower beds, and even a birch tree!

'There's Mum's bird feeder,' said Lindsay, pointing. The stand in the centre of the garden had a feeding-station on its top. Already dozens of birds were squabbling over its seeds, flapping and fluttering.

'You stay here,' whispered Twink. 'They'll fly away if they see you.' Suddenly she realised that this was farewell. She hovered uncertainly. 'Well – goodbye, Lindsay. Thank you for everything.'

'That's OK,' said Lindsay, struggling to smile. 'Goodbye, Twink – I'll never forget you.' She cracked open the conservatory door. Taking a deep breath, Twink flew outside.

Chapter Six

There were all sorts of birds gathered around the feeder, from magpies and starlings down to tiny little tits. And one of the tits was grey and yellow, just like Sunny!

Twink smiled. Tits might not be as powerful as larger birds, but if this one was anything like Sunny, he'd make up for it with his eagerness to please. She flew quickly to the bird feeder, landing on the perch beside him.

'Hello!' she said. The birds all stopped quarrelling and gaped at her. The tit looked astonished, puffing out its yellow chest feathers in alarm.

'Er . . . I'm sure you've all seen a fairy before,' said Twink, suddenly not sure at all. Maybe these birds had only ever seen humans. Still, fairies got on with all creatures – after all, taking care of nature was their job!

'I need a lift home,' continued Twink. She hesitated. Could the birds even understand her? 'It's miles and miles away, and I can't fly there on my own. So – can I ride on one of you?'

The birds rustled, glancing at each other. Twink looked directly at the tit. 'Will *you* help me?' she asked.

He cocked his head to one side, regarding her with dark, intelligent eyes.

'Please!' added Twink, moving closer to him. From the corner of her gaze, she could just see Lindsay, watching open-mouthed from the conservatory.

The tit didn't move away, and Twink studied his sleek grey back. She hadn't thought of the fact that there was no saddle. How would she hold on?

Well, there was only one way to find out. Twink fluttered just above the tit and settled herself behind his wings. His feathers felt smooth as glass. Holding on as best she could, Twink gave Lindsay a quick grin and a wave.

'Up!' she said, clutching the bird's neck.

The tit craned his head to stare at her. His expression didn't look very friendly.

'*Up,*' repeated Twink. She nudged him with her knees. 'Please!' she added. But the tit seemed to shrink sulkily in on himself, folding his wings tightly against his back. Nothing Twink could say or do would make him move.

Finally she climbed down from his back, red-cheeked. What a moss brain she must have looked! The moment she was off, the tit flew away as fast as he could. Twink sighed, and looked at the other birds.

Perhaps the magpie? It would be much harder to hold on to – they were so big! – but it would get her home even faster.

However, the magpie was an even worse disaster

than the tit had been. The moment he felt Twink sitting on his back, he gave an outraged '*Squaawwkkk!*' and rocketed straight up into the air. The other birds flapped away in a startled explosion.

'Aargh!' shrieked Twink, struggling to hang on. 'Stop!' The magpie shot up to the birch tree, and Twink ducked just in time to avoid being hit by a branch.

The bird plunged and dived wildly, clearly intent on throwing her off. It was like trying to ride a hurricane! With a yelp, Twink went tumbling through the air, arms and legs flailing.

In a flurry of wings, she caught herself and hovered, watching dejectedly as the magpie flapped away. The rest of the birds were gone as well, and the bird feeder looked sad and abandoned. Tears stung Twink's eyes. What *now*?

The back door opened and Lindsay ran outside, shivering in her thin nightdress.

'Twink, what happened?' she cried, holding out her hand.

Twink landed lightly on her palm. 'I – I suppose

the birds that we fly are specially trained. These don't seem to have the hang of it.' That was an understatement! If the situation hadn't been so serious, she'd have burst into giggles.

'Oh.' Lindsay looked troubled. 'Then . . . how are you going to get home?'

'I don't know,' Twink whispered. She rubbed her lavender wings together. 'Oh, Lindsay, I don't know!'

The next few days passed dismally for Twink. Though Lindsay did everything she could think of to cheer her up – bringing her delicious morsels to nibble, talking with her for hours, even playing games – all Twink could think of was her family, trying to find her.

'I know,' said Lindsay sympathetically. 'It must be awful.' She sighed. 'I've been trying and trying to get Dad to drive me to the farm, but he's told me not to nag him any more. And Mum says he means it, and that I should stop talking about it.'

Twink sighed. 'Well – thanks anyway.'

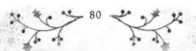

She was sitting on the first floor of the doll's house, with her legs dangling over the side. She and Lindsay had decided it was the safest place for her: if one of Lindsay's parents came in it would look like Lindsay was just playing with her dolls.

Now Lindsay gave Twink a sidelong look. 'Twink . . . can I ask you something?'

'Of course,' said Twink, stretching her wings. Apart from anything else, she was bored. She had never spent so long cooped up in one place in her life!

'Well . . .' Lindsay traced a finger on the carpet. 'You know what you told me about trees having personalities, and sometimes dryads? Is that really true?'

'Yes!' exclaimed Twink in surprise. 'And that's not all. Why, we have water sprites living in our school pond, and my father even met a faun once – though I think they're pretty rare now.'

Lindsay's eyes shone. 'There really *is* magic, isn't there? No matter what the grown-ups say.'

Twink swung her legs. 'The grown-ups in *my*

world would never say such a daft thing! Yes, of course there's magic.'

'That's what I've been trying to tell Dad,' said Lindsay. 'That maybe there really *is* magic, and maybe the trees are part of it, somehow, and so we shouldn't cut them down.' She sighed. 'But he doesn't seem to be listening.'

Impulsively, Twink flew out of the doll's house. 'Thank you for trying,' she said, brushing her wing against Lindsay's cheek. 'It means a lot, Lindsay – it really does!'

'That's OK,' said Lindsay, the tips of her ears turning bright red. 'But you know what, Twink?' she added. '*Christmas* is magic, too! It gives me the same sort of feeling that thinking about dryads does: all sort of tingly inside.'

Christmas was magic? Twink blinked in surprise. But humans didn't *have* magic. What was Lindsay talking about?

'Well –' She stopped, not wanting to hurt Lindsay's feelings.

'And it's almost here – tomorrow's Christmas Eve!'

82

Lindsay drummed her feet on the floor. 'Oh, I can hardly wait!'

Twink smiled, glad she hadn't said anything. She had no idea why Lindsay was so excited . . . but it was nice to see her friend happy!

That night Twink sat perched on the window sill long after Lindsay had fallen asleep, staring out at the dark houses. What was her family doing right now? Were they still searching for her, or had they given up? After all, days and days had passed – they might imagine she was gone for good by now.

No! She *couldn't* think like that, or else she'd give up entirely! Shoving the unpleasant thought away, Twink flitted to the bedroom door and listened. The house was silent. Slipping underneath the door, Twink flew downstairs and into the lounge.

'Hi, Clarence,' she whispered when the dog came padding over. He gave her a soft, companionable *woof*, wagging his tail.

Skimming across the darkened room to the tree, Twink landed beside the box-like thing that

controlled the lights. Using all her strength, she jumped as hard as she could on to the switch.

The tree erupted into a dazzle of sparkling white. Twink sank back on her heels, drinking it in as it flashed and glittered.

She wasn't really sure why she'd started sneaking downstairs to admire the tree. It had started when she couldn't sleep a few nights ago . . . and ever since then, she'd savoured the secret time that she spent down here. The tree was so beautiful – even if

84

she still didn't understand why the humans did it.

Flying up into the branches, Twink settled beside the fairy with holly-leaf wings and hugged her knees to her chest. Her parents must be so worried about her. If only she could get a message to them!

But how could she? Fairies always used butterflies to send messages to each other, but Twink knew they were specially chosen, sprinkled with fairy dust. Ordinary butterflies were all hibernating now. Getting a message to her family was hopeless!

Unless . . . Twink gasped as a memory came to her. When she'd been a first-year pupil, she'd befriended a wasp called Stripe, who had called to her with his mind when he'd needed help. Miss Shimmery, their HeadFairy, had explained it was the magic of friendship that made it possible.

Twink's heart beat wildly. Could *she* do the same thing? Maybe if she tried calling to Bimi, her best friend would hear her! Closing her eyes, Twink thought fervently, *Bimi, it's me! I'm trapped in a human house, but I'm all right. Please tell my parents that I'm OK, and I'm trying to get home!*

Over and over, Twink thought the words, sending them out with as much force as she could muster. She imagined Bimi receiving them, and the mix of relief and concern that would be on her best friend's face as she realised the trouble Twink was in.

Finally Twink stopped, holding her breath. She knew Bimi would certainly call back if she had heard her. *Please, Bimi, answer me*, she thought.

She waited for a long time, hopeful and alert. But

no answer came. There was only the slight sound of Clarence's snores, and the occasional sound of cars passing outside.

At last Twink's shoulders slumped in defeat. Well, that was that. And she had tried so hard! Maybe calling with your mind only worked between a fairy and a wasp.

Looking out of the window, Twink saw the winter stars fading from the sky. She must have been trying to call Bimi for ages. She tapped the fairy decoration, and watched her holly wings sparkle as she swung back and forth.

'Stupid of me, eh?' she whispered.

The painted fairy didn't respond. Twink sighed. It was back to the doll's house, then. And she might as well get used to it – it looked as if she was going to be living there for a long time!

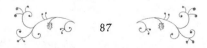

Chapter Seven

'I've got something for you,' said Lindsay.

Twink looked up. It was the next afternoon, and she was sitting perched on the doll's house chimney, trying not to feel sorry for herself.

'What?' she asked, managing a smile.

Lindsay drew a hand out from behind her back. 'Ta-da!' she said.

Twink's eyes widened. Lindsay was holding out a slim, gaily-wrapped package half as tall as Twink, decorated with a gleaming golden bow.

'What is it?' she asked in wonder.

'A Christmas present, silly!' Lindsay giggled. 'I know today's only Christmas Eve – but – oh, Twink, just open it!'

Maybe it was something to help her get home! Leaping to her feet, Twink held out both hands as Lindsay gave her the package – and then stared blankly at its clear, sticky fastening.

'Here, I'll do it!' cried Lindsay. She tore open the package as Twink fluttered beside her, craning to see. 'There!' said the girl with a triumphant grin.

Twink's spirits fell. It was only a comb – a tiny white one, made of that material called 'plastic'

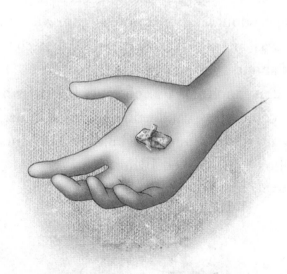

humans were so fond of. She smiled weakly. 'Lindsay, thank you! Where did you get it?'

'It's for one of my dolls,' explained Lindsay. 'I just found it again this morning. Here, try it!'

Though much too small for a human, Twink still had to use both hands to draw the comb through her long pink hair. Even so, it felt lovely to groom it – she had been feeling as scruffy as an old crow.

'Thanks, Lindsay,' she said again, meaning it this time. 'It was really nice of you to think of me.'

Lindsay sat cross-legged on the carpet as she watched Twink comb her hair. 'I just wish I could help you get home again,' she sighed. 'Oh, it's not fair. Wishes should always come true at Christmas!'

'They should?' Twink looked up with interest. This was an aspect of Christmas that she hadn't heard about.

Lindsay nodded. 'Yes, of course! Why, whenever Santa comes, he –' Suddenly she stopped, her hands flying up to her mouth. 'Twink, that's it! Santa!'

'Who's Santa?' asked Twink.

Lindsay's green-brown eyes grew wide. 'Santa

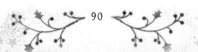

Claus! Don't you know? He's the spirit of Christmas!'

Wonder tickled across Twink's wings. 'He is?'

'Yes!' exclaimed Lindsay. 'Santa can do *anything*. All you have to do is wait up tonight and ask him to take you home again, and he'll do it, I know he will!'

Twink gaped at her. 'You mean he's coming *here*?'

Lindsay's words tumbled over each other as she explained about the red-suited, white-bearded man called Santa – also known as Father Christmas – who travelled to every human's house on Christmas Eve, delivering presents to all the children.

'*Flying reindeer?*' Twink felt as if her eyes might pop out of her head. She had never imagined such powerful magic!

Lindsay nodded vehemently. 'Yes, and the one who flies at the head of the sleigh is called Rudolph, and he has a red nose . . . though that bit might just be a story.' She made a face. 'My friend Sarah says it's *all* a story, but she's wrong. Santa comes every year, he really does!'

Hope fizzed through Twink like sparkling dew. 'But Lindsay, why haven't we fairies ever heard of Santa Claus?' she asked.

Lindsay shrugged. 'Maybe he's just for humans. But Twink, I'm *sure* he'll help you as well – he's ever so kind!'

Twink spent the rest of the day in an agony of anticipation. Wouldn't night-time *ever* come? The minute hand on Lindsay's clock was creeping as slowly as a snail!

But at last it arrived. After Lindsay's mother had said goodnight and closed her daughter's door, Twink flitted across the room and hovered near Lindsay's pillow. 'I'm going to sneak downstairs now,' she whispered.

She rubbed cold hands against her skirt. It frightened her to go downstairs when Lindsay's parents were still awake, but she didn't dare wait. What if Santa came and she missed him?

'I wish I could come with you,' Lindsay whispered back, propping herself up on one elbow. 'Oh, Twink, good luck! I really hope Santa takes you home.'

* * *

Twink sat hidden in the Christmas tree, tapping her wings together nervously. When would Santa come? And what on earth would she say to him when he did?

Lindsay's parents were sitting on one of the sofas, staring at a large box in the corner. Though Twink had kept carefully out of view as she sneaked through the room, she soon realised that she could have flown straight past them, singing and doing barrel rolls. They were far too entranced by the box to notice anything else!

Twink gazed in wonder at the box's moving pictures. Was it magic or something else? She had never seen anything like it! The figures in the box moved and spoke so fast that it made her dizzy.

Finally Lindsay's father stirred. 'Is it time for Santa yet?'

Twink jerked upright. It was really true, then! If even Lindsay's parents believed, then there *must* be such a being!

Lindsay's mother glanced towards the stairs.

'Lindsay might still be awake,' she said.

Lindsay's father stretched out his legs. 'Well, Santa can't come if little girls are still awake, can he?' The two of them fell into silence again, so that the only sound was the box.

Twink's heart galloped. Santa must be on his way right now! All she had to do was wait.

The story on the box ended, and another one began. Despite herself, Twink's anticipation turned to yawns. She'd hardly got any sleep the night before, when she'd stayed up so late trying to contact Bimi,

and now her eyelids felt as heavy as boulders.

Stifling another yawn, Twink nestled against the prickly branch and tucked her wings against her back. She wouldn't go to sleep, she promised herself drowsily. Not without meeting Santa. She wouldn't . . . she wouldn't . . .

'Look at me!' demanded a voice. Twink awoke with a gasp. The fairy decoration was hovering in front of her, beating her sparkly green wings.

'You're real!' exclaimed Twink, sitting up. 'But – but how –'

'Santa did it.' The fairy laughed, kicking her feet in the air. 'Santa can do anything!' she called as she skimmed away.

'Wait!' cried Twink. She started to fly from the tree, and then fell back with a yelp as a sudden blaze of light burst through the room. A tall figure in flowing red robes appeared.

Santa had arrived.

Twink cowered against her branch. The spirit of Christmas wasn't at all like Lindsay had described.

He was almost as tall as the ceiling! His long white beard looked wild and woodsy, with a jaunty holly bow and – Twink blinked in amazement – a pair of robins nesting in it!

Santa strode forward, his red robes swirling about his feet. A hush seemed to fall as he stooped beside the tree, placing presents under it. Twink watched in a daze. All thoughts of talking to him had vanished.

As Santa rose, he caught sight of Twink and smiled. 'Hello, little fairy,' he said gently. 'Don't worry, you'll see your family again – that's my Christmas promise to you! Now, hop on to my hand and I'll take you home.'

Joy burst through Twink. She leapt towards Santa's outstretched hand – and then suddenly she was flying through her old familiar meadow, enjoying the winter chill on her wings.

She was really back! There were trees, and grass, and open spaces. With a shout of delight, Twink did a midair somersault, and then sped towards her family's tree stump. How excited everyone would be to see her!

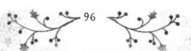

* * *

Twink smiled in her sleep. Home . . . everyone was so happy . . . but something was wrong. What was it?

Sleepily, she opened her eyes – and then jolted wide awake. The room was dark! Lindsay's parents were gone. Only the soft sound of Clarence's snores filled the air. Beside her, Twink could just make out the little fairy – a dangling decoration once more.

It was only a dream! Twink slumped against the branch as disappointment crashed through her.

But . . . maybe Santa hadn't come yet. Surely her dream meant that he *would* come and save her. Twink dived from the tree and plunged downwards to the little box that controlled the lights.

Click! The tree burst into sparkles as she landed on the switch. Twink held her breath, looking around her. And then she saw it, and her wings drooped in dismay.

A new pile of brightly wrapped presents was clustered under the tree. Dejectedly, Twink flew from one to the other, peering at the cards. They all said

exactly what she'd known they'd say: *To Lindsay, with love from Santa Claus.*

Santa had already come and gone.

Twink sank on to the large golden bow of the last present, fighting tears. Oh, *how* could she have been so stupid as to fall asleep? This had been her last chance!

And now she was too late.

Chapter Eight

'Mum! Dad! I love it!' A pile of crumpled wrapping paper lay beside Lindsay, revealing a pink satin jewellery box.

'Look inside,' said her father, smiling.

Tired and sad as she was, Twink felt a tremor of excitement as Lindsay opened the lid, craning to see from her hiding place in Clarence's wicker basket. It smelled strongly of dog, but apart from that was surprisingly cosy – especially since Clarence seemed very protective of Twink now, and insisted on cradling her with the curve of his tail!

The little girl squealed with delight as she held up a tiny golden locket. 'Mum, Dad, thank you!' she cried, launching herself at her parents for a hug.

A warm glow filled Twink as she watched. Lindsay had said that Christmas wasn't supposed to be about presents, and she was right. It was about *family* – and that was something that both fairies and humans could understand.

Twink sighed and stroked Clarence's soft black fur. Oh, how she wished that she could see her own family again! But Santa's Christmas promise had only been a dream. What would her friends at Glitterwings Academy think when the new term started and she wasn't there? They'd all be so worried!

Lindsay had been very sympathetic when she'd woken that morning and realised that Twink was still trapped. The little girl had brought Twink a small piece of something called 'toast' with honey on it.

'I'm sort of glad that you're still here for Christmas, though,' she'd confessed as Twink ate. 'Oh, Twink, you have to come downstairs and see! Mum and Dad are up; it's almost time to open our presents!'

Twink had shrugged, wiping honey off her mouth. 'I suppose so,' she said glumly. Frankly, she thought she'd had enough of Christmas to last her a lifetime. It had already got her into more trouble than she'd ever dreamed of!

But Lindsay seemed so eager that Twink didn't have the heart to refuse. So the little girl had sneaked Twink downstairs in the pocket of her dressing gown, and tucked her securely into Clarence's basket when her parents weren't looking.

And now Twink couldn't take her eyes off what was happening! Lindsay had been right. Christmas *was* magic. The family's love for each other, and the beauty of the tree, and the excitement of the presents – it all came together to make a spell as magical as anything the fairies had ever done.

When the presents were all unwrapped, Lindsay's mother brought out biscuits and hot chocolate. 'Isn't this nice?' she said, stretching out on the floor. 'We should do this more often.'

'Hey, why not? We could have Christmas twice a year!' laughed Lindsay's dad. 'Let's do it again in

June, with all the trimmings.'

'No!' said Lindsay in alarm. 'We can't cut down *more* trees.'

Her father groaned, scraping his hair back. 'Oh, here we go again. Lindsay, love, I was only joking.'

'It's true, though,' said Lindsay stubbornly. She put down her biscuit. 'We *shouldn't* have cut down the tree. It has dryads and things living it, and – and feelings, and –'

'That's it!' said Lindsay's father, standing up. 'It's time!' He strode from the room.

Lindsay looked stricken. Her mother patted her hand. 'Don't worry – there's a surprise for you!'

A surprise? Twink stretched her neck to see. There was the sound of the back door closing, and then Lindsay's father came back into the room. Twink gasped. He was holding a *tree*! He really was – a baby spruce tree, in a bright green pot that had a red bow tied around it.

'Merry Christmas, my little eco-warrior,' he laughed, handing the tiny tree to Lindsay. 'Am I forgiven now for chopping down the tree?'

'Oh, *Dad*,' whispered Lindsay. A huge smile spread across her face as she touched one of the tree's bristly branches. 'I love it. It's my favourite present of all!' She flung herself at her father, hugging him around his middle.

Lindsay's mother beamed. 'We thought we'd all go to Uncle Matt's farm this spring and plant it – to make up for the other one, since you seem so worried about it!'

Uncle Matt's farm! That was where home was! Twink froze as hope tingled through her.

'Oh! Can't we go now?' screeched Lindsay. She jumped up and down, tugging at her father's arms. 'Please, please! We need to go *now*, we really do!'

'*Lind*-say,' groaned her father. 'For one thing, it's not the right time of year to plant trees, and for another it's Christmas Day and I've no intention of driving all the way out there –'

'Oh, please! It's so important!' Lindsay whirled towards her mum. '*Can* we, Mum? Please?'

'*Now?*' Lindsay's mother shook her head. 'Oh, Lindsay –'

'*Please*,' begged Lindsay again, clasping her hands under her chin. She turned from one parent to the other. 'Please! It's all I want!'

There was a pause as her mother and father looked at each other. In the basket, Twink hardly dared to move. Even Clarence seemed to be holding his breath.

'I suppose we really should have seen this coming,' said Lindsay's father, rolling his eyes. 'Oh, I don't know. What do you think, Karen?'

Lindsay's mother sighed, and shrugged her slim shoulders. 'Well . . . the turkey's in the oven, so we

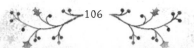

have a few hours before anything else needs doing. And the traffic won't be too bad, at least.'

'No, because everyone who's sensible will be staying at home, enjoying Christmas!' grumbled Lindsay's father. 'OK, kiddo, you've got your wish,' he said as Lindsay burst into squeals of delight. 'I'll ring Matt and let him know we're coming.'

'Oh! I'm going home!' burst out Twink in a joyous whisper, hugging Clarence's tail. Its furry tip thumped as Clarence gave a soft, friendly *woof*.

And on the Christmas tree, the fairy decoration seemed to smile.

Twink spent her second car journey tucked in Lindsay's soft, fleecy pocket. The strange motion of the car made her feel just as ill as before, but this time she was too excited to care. She was going home! She was really going to see her family again, just as Santa had promised!

Finally the vehicle stopped, and she felt Lindsay get out of the car. There were crunching footsteps as the family headed into the woods.

Twink's heart raced. She could smell the evergreens, and the sharp tang of snow! It was all she could do not to dart out of Lindsay's pocket and fly home that very moment – but of course she had to say goodbye to Lindsay before she left.

Twink felt a pang at the thought of it. She would never have imagined that she could be friends with a human . . . but that's exactly what she and Lindsay had become. Still – still, maybe they could see each other again, somehow.

The footsteps stopped. 'Well, here's the scene of the crime,' said Lindsay's father.

'Lindsay, shall we plant the new tree here, beside where the old one was cut down?' asked her mother brightly.

'Yes, please,' said Lindsay in a small voice. Twink realised that she was feeling sad, too, and her own heart ached. How was it possible to be so happy and so miserable at the same time?

The sound of digging began. 'Oof! The ground's hard as a rock,' said Lindsay's father. 'Karen, can you clear away that stone for me?'

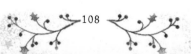

Just when Twink was starting to fidget with impatience, there was a rush of fresh air as Lindsay's pocket opened. The little girl peeked inside, her cheeks pink with the cold. 'We're here,' she whispered.

'I – I know,' said Twink.

She flew out of Lindsay's pocket and hovered in front of the girl. They were in a snowy forest glade, and Twink's spirits leapt as she recognised it. Her home was only a few minutes' flight away!

Lindsay's parents were both busy digging the hole, their backs to Lindsay. Twink cleared her throat. 'Well . . . I suppose it's time for me to go.'

'Oh, I wish you didn't have to!' cried Lindsay. Her brown-green eyes shone with tears. 'I'm really going to miss you, Twink.'

'What was that, sweetie?' asked Lindsay's mother, looking over her shoulder. Her jaw dropped as she caught sight of Twink. 'Tom!' she gasped, grabbing her husband's arm. 'It's that moth again!'

Lindsay's father turned and stared at Twink in disbelief. 'It can't be! It must be some other moth.'

'It's not a moth at all!' burst out Lindsay. 'She's a

fairy – can't you see?'

Her mother laughed uncertainly. 'Lindsay, don't be silly. There's no such thing.'

'There *is*,' insisted Lindsay. Her face flushed bright red. 'She's lived in my doll's house for over a week now, and you didn't even know! That's why we had to come here, to bring her home again.'

'But – but it *can't* be . . .' Lindsay's father trailed off as he gaped at Twink.

'Oh my goodness,' murmured Lindsay's mother, her eyes wide. 'Tom, I know it's mad, but . . . I really think it *is* one.'

As if in a dream, both parents drew slowly forward. Twink bobbed in the air, ready to dart away at the first sign of moth-swatting.

But when Lindsay's parents were stood beside their daughter, they simply stared at Twink, their eyes round as oranges. Twink licked her lips, looking back at them. They didn't have to stare *quite* so hard, did they? She felt like one of the animals in Mr Woodleaf's Creature Kindness class!

Suddenly Lindsay fumbled in her other pocket.

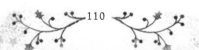

'Oh, I almost forgot! Here's your comb, Twink – and I've got something else for you, as well.' She held out the comb, along with a tiny package. 'Don't open it until later,' she said. 'It's a surprise.'

Twink took the items, cradling them in her arms. 'Thank you, Lindsay,' she said softly. 'I – I'll never forget you.'

'I'll never forget you either,' choked out Lindsay. She swiped at her eyes. 'Oh, I don't mean to cry! I'm happy that you're going home, Twink, I really am.'

'I know,' said Twink. She flitted upwards and gently brushed a wing against Lindsay's damp cheek. 'Thanks for everything, Lindsay. I hope we'll get to see each other again some day.'

Lindsay caught her breath. 'Maybe we could!' She whirled towards her parents. 'Mum, Dad, we could come back, couldn't we? Sometime when Twink is home, visiting her parents?'

'Her . . . parents?' mumbled Lindsay's father. He swallowed hard. 'Do – do fairies really have . . . ?'

'Well, of course!' said Lindsay in exasperation. 'Mum, can we? *Please?*'

'Yes – yes, we'll come back,' murmured Lindsay's mother with a soft smile. 'I mean – we'd be honoured to meet your parents,' she added to Twink. She put an arm around her husband. 'Wouldn't we, dear?'

Lindsay's father nodded dazedly. 'Yes, we would.'

A sunny glow spread through Twink as she and the adult humans regarded each other. 'Thank you,' she said shyly. 'I'm sure they'd like to meet you, too.'

'Hurrah!' cried Lindsay, bouncing on her toes. 'Have a great time when you get back to school, Twink – send me a butterfly!'

'I will,' grinned Twink. So far as she knew, the school butterflies had never delivered a message to a human before – but there was no reason why they couldn't!

Waving over her shoulder, Twink skimmed off across the glade. The last glimpse she had of Lindsay was the little girl jumping up and down, waving back as hard as she could. But her parents simply stood with their arms around each other, staring after Twink in wonder.

'Mum, Dad, I'm home!' shouted Twink, bursting into the stump. 'Teena! Bimi! I'm here!'

Her words rang emptily through the house. Twink hovered, holding the plastic comb and Lindsay's package to her chest. 'Mum? Dad?' she called again.

Where *was* everyone? Dropping her things on the mushroom table, Twink flitted through the rooms – her comfy bedroom with its rose-petal bedcover, her parents' room, the cosy kitchen.

But the stump was empty.

Disappointment trembled through her. Twink slumped into the mossy armchair, fighting tears. What *now*? She had been longing so much to see her family again – it had never occurred to her that they wouldn't be here!

Wiping her eyes, Twink glanced morosely around the stump – and spotted a petal on the table. Leaping across the room, she snatched it up.

Dearest Twink,
If you somehow manage to return and read this note,

*we've gone to try and find you. Just wait for us here,
and we'll be back as soon as we can.*

Lots of love,
Mum and Dad

Twink's throat clenched. They hadn't given up
on her after all! But when had they left? How long
ago?

Twink dropped the petal and shot from the
stump. Maybe she had only just missed them! If she
hurried –

The field stretched around her, snowy and silent.
Twink spun in midair, scanning it wildly. 'Mum,
Dad!' she called, cupping her hands around her
mouth. 'Teena! Where are you?'

But there was nothing, not even a bird.

After a while Twink stopped shouting, and
hovered forlornly. Oh, it was hopeless! That note
had probably been written days ago. She'd just have
to wait, even though the ache to see her family again
felt like agony.

Her spirits heavy, Twink turned to go back inside

. . . and then she saw something out of the corner of her eye.

'Oh!' she gasped in delight. There was a hawk flying across the frozen stream, with a group of fairies riding on its back! The fairies hadn't spotted her yet, and their wings looked weary and defeated.

'Mum, Dad!' she screamed. She flew towards the hawk as fast as she could, her pink hair whistling behind her. 'I'm here!' she shouted. 'I'm here!'

The fairies looked up. It was her parents and Teena! And Bimi and *her* parents were alongside them! Her heart singing, Twink put on an extra burst of speed. Her parents leapt off the hawk's back and flew towards her, calling her name.

And then all at once she was there with them, scooped up in their arms. 'Mum, Dad!' she sobbed. 'I'm so glad to see you!'

'Oh, Twink, you're safe!' cried her mother.

'Don't ever go missing again, Twinkster,' whispered her father raggedly. 'I don't think we could take the strain!'

That night the tree stump rang with laughter as the fairies sat up talking, overjoyed at being reunited. Twink sat nestled between her parents, munching a slice of her mum's delicious honey cake – which Mum had insisted on baking the moment they got inside! – and feeling happier than she'd ever been.

Bimi *had* got Twink's message, as it turned out. 'I was so relieved!' she said, her blue eyes wide with the memory. 'None of us knew *what* had happened to you. I tried and tried to respond, but I suppose you didn't hear me.'

Twink shook her head. 'I thought *you* hadn't heard *me*,' she said sheepishly.

Bimi explained that she'd returned to her own home the day after Twink had disappeared – but her parents had brought her straight back to Twink's when she told them about the message.

'We knew it was important the moment Bimi told us,' said Twink's mother, giving Bimi a warm smile. 'So we asked her and her parents to come with us while we looked for you, in case you contacted her

again with more details.'

'We didn't realise that you were so far away,' added Twink's father. 'We've been searching nearby neighbourhoods and villages for days, casting every spell we could think of to try and find you!'

'I'm glad I didn't know,' said Twink's mum with a shudder. 'Fifty miles! I would have been even more worried than I already was.'

Twink's cheeks grew hot. 'I – I'm sorry, Mum,' she said guiltily. 'I should have listened to you about the tree.'

'Never mind, Twinkster,' said her dad, ruffling her hair. 'Maybe you disobeyed, but we're proud of you for trying to do the right thing. You and Bimi are both pretty amazing girls, you know!' Bimi and Twink grinned across the room at each other in relief.

'But Twink, tell us about being in the human house!' said Teena, her violet eyes wide. 'Weren't you scared?'

'At first,' said Twink. As her family and friends listened, Twink shared her adventures, and told about her friendship with Lindsay – and attempted

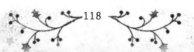

118

to describe Christmas, though it was difficult to put into words the magic she had felt.

'Why, it sounds lovely,' said Mrs Bluebell in surprise. 'Who would have thought that the humans would have such a tradition?'

'Maybe they're not so different from us after all,' said Twink's mother thoughtfully.

Twink's story of Santa Claus was met with even more astonishment. 'What a powerful spirit!' exclaimed Bimi's father. 'I can't imagine why we've never heard of him.'

Twink's own father nodded as he sipped his cup of hot nectar. 'We'll have to inform Queen Mab of this,' he said gravely. 'I'm sure she'll want to make contact with him.'

Twink felt a solemn thrill as she remembered her dream. Wouldn't it be wonderful if the fairies and Santa could work together, somehow? Why, perhaps they could even go riding in his magical sleigh!

'It's all so strange,' breathed Bimi, curled up beside her own parents. 'But Twink, I still don't understand why the humans cut trees down, just to water and decorate them. It doesn't make any sense.' She and the others had listened open-mouthed as Twink described the Christmas tree in all its sparkling finery.

'I know,' said Twink slowly. 'I don't understand it either, except . . . except I think they *do* love nature in their way, and magic, too. Why, they call the sparkling lights "fairy lights", and there was even a fairy decoration on the tree!'

There were murmurs of amazement. Twink went on, struggling to find the words. 'I think . . . I think maybe Christmas trees are a way for humans to have a bit of magic in their lives. They're so cut off from everything in their houses. It's like they're longing for something, but don't even realise it . . .' She trailed off in confusion, realising that the stump had gone quiet.

Twink's father squeezed her shoulder. 'Maybe so,' he said gently. 'But you're not allowed to go chasing after any more trees to find out!'

Later, as the fairies munched the last of the honey cake, Twink's plastic comb was passed about and exclaimed over. 'How glimmery!' giggled Teena, pulling it through her own shining hair. 'Can I borrow it sometimes, Twink?'

All at once Twink remembered Lindsay's other present. 'Oh, I almost forgot!' she gasped. Grabbing it from the table, she excitedly tore off the red wrapping as the others crowded around her.

'What is it?' cried Bimi, craning to see.

For a moment Twink stared . . . and then she burst out laughing. 'It's a piece of chocolate,' she grinned, holding it up. 'You're all going to love this – it's even better than honey cake!'

The chocolate was duly shared out. 'Delicious!' pronounced Twink's father, licking his fingers. 'I think my whole opinion of humans is changing.'

'Mum, can I have some more?' begged Teena, fluttering her wings.

'No, that's all there is,' laughed Twink's mother, guiding her younger daughter from the room. 'Besides, it's your bedtime!'

As the adults chatted, Twink and Bimi smiled at each other. There were no words needed. Twink was the luckiest fairy in the world, and she knew it. She was home again, back with her family where she belonged. And in just a few days she and Bimi would return to Glitterwings Academy, where she'd have so many adventures to tell.

But best of all, she had a new friend: a little girl named Lindsay, who knew now that fairies were real . . . and who had taught Twink about the magic of Christmas.

Twink smiled, picturing Lindsay in her pink and white bedroom. Oh, she hoped that she'd get to see her again some day.

Merry Christmas, Lindsay, thought Twink, meaning the words with all her heart. *And thank you!*

READ ON FOR SOME GLIMMERY FAIRY ACTIVITIES!

Twink's Top Tips for a Recycled Christmas

1. I noticed these things called *Christmas cards* when I was in Lindsay's house . . . and they're so pretty that I wondered why you humans don't save them to use as Christmas tree decorations. Why not ask your parents if they have any old cards from last year that they don't want any more? If they do, maybe they'll let you cut out nice designs from them – like Santa, or Christmas trees, or robins. You can decorate these even more with sparkly glitter or sequins if you like. Then just glue a ribbon to the back, and hey presto – home-made tree decorations!

2. One thing that Lindsay's mum was *always* getting cross about was the number of advertising leaflets that came through their door every day. (When I found out that the paper in them comes from trees, it made me cross as well!) But the colours in them are usually really pretty . . . so why not make them into paper chains for your tree? Cut them into strips, get out the glue or sticky tape and put the chains together. Loads of fun, and eco-friendly, too.

3. Finally . . . why not think about having a Christmas tree with a root ball so that you can plant it outside after the holidays, instead of one that's been chopped down? We fairies will thank you for it!

Merry Christmas!

Place a thin piece of paper over the picture of me below. Hold the paper in place and carefully draw around me. Remove the paper from the page and have fun decorating my outfit.

You could try:
- colouring me with pencils, crayons or paint
- sticking pieces of material, coloured paper or foil to my dress
- adding glitter to my wings to make them really twinkle!

Twink's Festive Treats

After tasting chocolate for the first time, I came up with the idea of mixing it with some of my favourite fairy food ingredients, like scrummy oats and honey. Here's my recipe for Festive Treats so you, your friends and family can enjoy them too. Yum!

You will need a responsible adult to help you make these!

100 g butter + a little extra
  to grease the cake tin
100 g demerara sugar
350 g oats
1 banana

3 tablespoons honey
50 g sultanas
1 teaspoon mixed spice
200 g milk chocolate
  (optional)

You'll also need a large saucepan, a cake tin 20 cm x 30 cm, a smaller pan and a glass bowl to fit snugly on top, a wooden spoon, a metal spoon and measuring scales to weigh out the ingredients (g = grams)

1. Set the oven to 180°C/350°F/Gas Mark 4.
2. Melt the butter in a large saucepan over a very low heat.
3. Add the demerara sugar, honey and mixed spice and mix well using the wooden spoon.

4. Mix together the sultanas and oats and stir them into the melted butter mixture. You'll find it easier adding a little at a time. Make sure all the oats are covered in the mixture.

5. Mash the banana to a liquid pulp and mix into the oats mixture. Make sure the oats, banana and sultanas are well mixed together.

6. Rub a little butter around the cake tin and spoon in the mixture. Press down with the back of a spoon, ensuring it is evenly spread and about 4 cm deep.

7. Place on to the middle shelf of the oven and bake for 15–18 minutes, until the edges are just turning golden brown.

8. Take out and set to one side to cool.

If you want to make a chocolate topping, break the chocolate into chunks and carefully melt it in the glass bowl over a pan of simmering water, ensuring the bowl does not touch the water. Keep stirring the chocolate until it is fully melted. Then spread the melted chocolate over the cooled oats mixture, using the back of the metal spoon to make it nice and even.

Leave the Festive Treats to cool for half an hour, then cut into slices and share with your best friend!

If you enjoyed this
special Christmas tale,
I'm sure you'll adore my
other glimmery stories.

Look out for more brand new Glitterwings Academy
adventures in Spring 2009, and make sure you visit
www.glitterwingsacademy.co.uk for fabulous fairy fun!